This edition first published in 2000
by Cat's Whiskers
96 Leonard Street, London EC2A 4XD

Cat's Whiskers Australia
14 Mars Road, Lane Cove, NSW 2066

ISBN 1 90301 219 8

o Hachette Livre 1999
English text o Cat's Whiskers 2000

A CIP catalogue record for this book is
available from the British Library

Printed in France by Pollina s.a. - n° L80145.Ae

Lily
Goes on a Plane

ANNE GUTMAN · GEORG HALLENSLEBEN

CAT'S Whiskers

THE WATTS PUBLISHING GROUP LTD

Guess where I was last week?

In a huge plane, high above the ocean.

I was travelling on my own, for the first time ever.

At first there was a lady sitting next to me.
"Don't be frightened," she told me,
"and try not to wriggle around so much."

"But it's the plane that's moving, not me!"
I said. In the end she changed seats,
I'm not quite sure why.

After the lady-in-blue had gone, I had
two seats all to myself!
I stretched out and had a really nice nap,
but not for long...

The stewardess woke
me up with a big
tray of goodies:
it was time to eat.

There were lots of things on the tray:

a glass

beef stew with carrots and peas

a plastic knife, fork and spoon

salt

soft cheese

pepper

water in a plastic container

a white roll

a pack of butter

cherry jam

an empty cup

and a **giant** orange juice

Then a voice said: "Ladies and gentlemen...

...please put on your headphones
for our film, Paradise Island."
But I had a problem!

From my seat, I could hardly see a thing.

Luckily, I had an idea.
I found a really good way
to watch the film,
even if...

...it wasn't very **comfortable.** The story was great, but unfortunately I missed the end because...

...I slipped on my glass.
DISASTER!
The glass was still full,
and the orange juice
spilled everywhere.

The stewardess came up. She seemed to be laughing!
"Don't worry," she said. "We'll tidy this up.
What's your name?"
"Lily," I replied. But I couldn't hear very well;
my ears were full of orange juice.
It was funny having a bath on a plane!
Afterwards the stewardess said, "Come with me,
Lily, I've got a surprise for you..."

She took me to the flight deck!
There were little coloured buttons
everywhere, even on the ceiling.
I wasn't allowed to touch them, but the
pilot told me what everything was for.
"You smell very nice," he said.
It must have been the soap.

When I got back to my seat, I could see twinkling lights
and lots of skyscrapers through the window.
From this high up, everything looked so tiny!
But it's true, the soap did have a nice smell.

And that's how I arrived in America,
clean and sweet-smelling.
I recognised my uncle straightaway:
he was holding up a board with my name on it.
We phoned my parents, but we forgot
that the time was different and
woke them up in the middle of the night.
"It doesn't matter, Lily," said my father.
"Have a good time in New York!"